COMING HOME
BOOK 2

D1003596

SEARCHING FOR ANSWERS

P J Gray

SADDLEBACK
EDUCATIONAL PUBLISHING

COMING HOME
BOOK 2

COMING HOME

SEARCHING FOR ANSWERS

THE TRUTH

SADDLEBACK
EDUCATIONAL PUBLISHING
www.sdlback.com

ISBN-13: 978-1-62250-052-9
ISBN-10: 1-62250-052-0
eBook: 978-1-61247-710-7

Printed in the U.S.A.

19 18 17 16 15   2 3 4 5 6

Author Acknowledgments

I wish to thank Carol Senderowitz for her friendship and belief in my abilities. I wish to thank Linnea Johnson for her inspiration and dedication to learning. Additional thanks and gratitude to my family and friends for their love and support; likewise to the staff at Saddleback Educational Publishing for their generosity, graciousness, and enthusiasm. Most importantly, my heartfelt thanks to Scott Drawe for his love and support.

Sadness

It had been four months since
Mike Baldwin was shot and killed.

Nia was sad all of the time.

She still could not cope with his death.

Nia cried almost every day.

She had loved him for many years.
But she could not tell anyone.

After church, Nia asked her friend Gail to come over for lunch.

Gail had lived next door for more than sixteen years.

She and Nia were best friends.

Gail knew that Nia's life had been hard.

Gail thought that Nia's son, Will, had made her life harder.

Nia and Gail had many things in common.

Gail also had a son. His name was Carl.

Carl worked for a computer company.
He traveled around the world.

Carl's wife left him after giving birth to their daughter, Jada.

Jada lived with Gail while Carl traveled.

She was five years old.

Gail and Nia fed Jada some lunch.

After Jada ate lunch, she watched TV while Gail and Nia talked.

Gail was the only person who knew about Nia's love for Mike.

She tried to make Nia feel better.

"Please don't cry," Gail begged.

"I am trying to cope, but I can't help it," Nia said.

They were both crying.

"Why did he have to die?" Nia asked.

"I'm so sorry," Gail said.

Gail held Nia's hand and wiped her tears as she cried.

Something Inside

Karyn and Will had become closer since Mike's death.

They liked to eat at a place called the Burger Joint.

They were happy spending time with each other.

Karyn was happy when she made Will smile.

But sometimes Will would get mad quickly and without warning.

Will still blamed Shawn for Mike's death.

"I know it was Shawn," Will said while eating his cheeseburger.

"But you said that the gunshots came from a big silver car," Karyn said.

"Yes, a silver car with black windows," Will said.

"Shawn does not drive a silver car," Karyn answered. "Will, you have to let the police handle this."

She looked down at her food and became very quiet.

She was scared that Will would find Shawn.

"He'll pay for what he did to my father," Will said under his breath.

Karyn said, "I don't want you to start anything. I don't want you to get hurt."

"I won't get hurt," Will said.

Karyn began to cry.

"I want our baby to have a father!" Karyn said quickly.

"Baby?"

In the Movies

Karyn returned to her job at the nail shop after her lunch with Will.

Eve, her boss, came out of the back room.

"I have great news!" Eve said. "A movie company wants to use my nail shop in their new movie."

Everyone in the shop was quiet.

"What is wrong with you girls? They are going to make a big movie here," Eve said.

She started to get mad.

"What about my customers?" asked one of the workers. "I'll lose money that day."

"No," Eve said. "All of you will be in the movie. All of you will get paid."

Everyone in the shop smiled at each other and laughed.

Eve said, "I will get the only speaking part. The movie director said so."

Suddenly the shop telephone rang.

Eve ran to the back room before picking up the call.

One of Karyn's co-workers wrapped a towel on her head.

She stood up and said, "Girls! It looks like Eve is going to be a big movie star!"

Everyone laughed.

Karyn also laughed as she walked into the bathroom.

Karyn could hear Eve on the telephone from the other side of the bathroom wall.

"Shawn is gone," Eve said to the caller. "I told him to leave town for now. The police are still asking questions about the shooting at the factory."

The Lie and the Truth

Will did not spend much time at home since Mike was killed.

Nia made Will's favorite dinner of chicken and rice.

She was happy that he stayed home for dinner.

Nia started talking about Mike.

She wanted Will to know the truth.

"Mike and I went to high school together," Nia said. "A few years later, we started working at the factory and fell in love."

"You always told me that my father was dead," Will said.

"I lied to you. I'm sorry," she said.

"Why did you lie, Mama?"

Nia said, "Mike couldn't marry me. He was already married."

She began to cry.

Will said nothing. He looked down at his food.

They sat. Nothing was said for a long time.

Nia wiped her tears.

"When will I meet your girlfriend?" Nia asked.

Will said nothing.

He did not want to tell Nia about the baby.

Will said, "I don't know when you'll meet her.
Why should I let you meet her, Mama?
You lied to me for so many years."

Will stood up, grabbed his coat, and walked
out of the house.

One Star Down

On Monday, the movie company came to the nail shop.

Everyone at the shop was happy.
They wore their best outfits.

Eve asked the director, "When will I get to speak in the movie?"

"You have to wait. First we have to set up the camera and the lights," the director replied.

They waited hours for the cameras and the lights to be placed.

Everyone was tired and mad.

Eve yelled at the director, "This is taking too long!"

The director asked Karyn, "What's your name?"

"It's Karyn," she answered.

"You're very pretty. Would you like the speaking part in the movie?" he asked.

"Yes," Karyn replied.

The director moved Karyn to the front and Eve to the back.

"I want Karyn to have your speaking part," the director said to Eve.

"That's fine with me," Eve said with a smile. "I will be right back."

Eve hurried down the basement steps.

She stood in the basement and screamed.

She hated Karyn.

At the end of the day, the director was happy.

He said, "Good job, everybody. Good job."

Before he left the shop, he asked Karyn, "Would you like to go to dinner with me?"

"No, thank you," Karyn replied. "I have a boyfriend."

"I don't care," he said.

Karyn watched him get into a big silver car and drive away.

A New Job and a New Friend

Will lost his job in the factory mail room after Mike died.

He never liked that job.

Will got a new job at another factory.

Will liked this job. He liked to work with his hands.

He made bathroom parts at the factory.

Will made a friend at the factory.

His name was Toby.

Toby worked next to Will.

They talked and laughed during work.

They also ate lunch together.

In his free time, Toby liked to buy old cars.

He fixed the old cars and sold them to make extra money.

"Let me hook you up with a new set of wheels," Toby said to Will.

Will was saving his money to buy a car from Toby.

Will liked to take Karyn out after work.

They liked to go to the Burger Joint.

They also liked to go to the movies.

Karyn did not want to tell Will about her part in the movie.

She did not want to tell him about the movie director.

She was scared.

Will kept looking for the big silver car.

Grandmother Nia

Karyn was happy to see Nia return to the nail shop.

Karyn liked Nia very much.

She still did not know that Nia was Will's mother.

"You seem very happy," Nia said.

"I am happy," Karyn replied.

"Why?"

Karyn moved closer to Nia.

"I'm going to have a baby," Karyn said quietly.

Nia could not speak. Her heart became warm.

Nia wanted to hug Karyn. But she didn't.

"Have you told your boyfriend?" Nia asked.

"Yes, ma'am. He knows."

Nia's eyes opened wide.

"Are you okay?" Karyn asked. "You look like you saw a ghost."

"I am fine, dear. Do you want to marry him?" Nia asked.

"Yes, I think so."

"Does he want to get married?" Nia asked.

"I don't know."

"You should tell him that you want to get married," Nia said with tears in her eyes.

"I will," Karyn replied.

HAPPY
BIRTHDAY

The Birthday Cake

Gail baked Nia a birthday cake.

They sat together in Gail's kitchen.

Gail said, "Happy birthday, Nia!"

Jada sat on Gail's lap.

Jada clapped her hands.

"Thank you, Gail. How is your son, Carl?" Nia asked.

"He's fine. He keeps so busy with his job. And he travels too much."

"Does he send you money for Jada?" Nia asked.

"Yes, but I wish he would come home soon. We miss him so much."

Nia nodded.

"Nia, do you have a birthday wish?" Gail asked.

"My wish has come true," Nia said.

"What do you mean?" Gail asked.

"I am going to be a grandmother!"

Gail asked, "Are you sure? When did Will tell you?"

"Will did not tell me. His girlfriend told me."

"His girlfriend?" Gail asked. "Nia, tell me everything, or I won't let you leave this room!"

Nia laughed at Gail. She began to tell her all about Karyn.

Nia told Gail about finding the nail shop where Karyn worked and their secret friendship.

"Cake! Cake! Cake!" Jada said as she clapped her hands.

Gail and Nia smiled at each other.

Gail cut the birthday cake.

It was bright pink and very sweet.

Gail asked Nia, "Will you tell Karyn who you are?"

"I will tell Karyn next week when I go back to the nail shop."

The Fall

It was a Wednesday afternoon.

The work day was over.

Karyn and Eve were the only workers left in the nail shop.

"I am going now," Eve said. "You have to put the dirty towels downstairs in the basement."

Karyn said, "Okay, I will. Then I'll go."

"Okay, Karyn," Eve replied. "Don't forget to lock up."

Karyn heard the back door close.

She gathered all of the dirty towels in her arms.

The dirty towels had to go to the basement for washing.

There were so many towels.

Karyn could not use her hands to open the basement door.

So she pushed the basement door open with her right foot.

Karyn stood at the top of the stairs.

The basement below was very dark.

Karyn could not see in front of her.

She tried to turn on the light as she stepped down.

Suddenly Karyn felt a hand on her back.

The hand pushed her.

Karyn fell forward down the stairs.

The towels flew up into the air.

Karyn kept falling down the stairs.

Her body hit each step.

Her arms scraped the walls.

Her legs, back, and head bumped on every step. *Thunk. Thunk. Thunk.*

She landed on the basement floor.

Karyn's body did not move. Her eyes were closed.

The Answer

Will sat in his car.

He waited for Karyn to finish work.

He was parked across the street from the nail shop.

Will looked at car magazines and listened to music.

He looked at his watch. Then he looked at the shop.

He could see through the front window.

He could not see Karyn in the shop.

Suddenly a big silver car drove away from the back of the shop.

Will knew that it was *the* car.

It was the same car from the day Mike was killed.

Will wanted to follow the car.

He looked at the shop window again.

He could not see Karyn.

Then Will saw Nia walking down the street.

Will watched the car drive away.

He watched his mother walk into the nail shop.

He could not understand why Nia was there.

"Does Mama know Karyn?" he asked himself.

Will could not wait for Karyn.

He had to follow the car.

About the Author

PJ Gray is a versatile, award-winning freelance writer experienced in short stories, essays, and feature writing. He is a former managing editor for *Pride* magazine, a ghost writer, blogger, researcher, food writer, and cookbook author. He currently resides in Chicago, Illinois. For more information about PJ Gray, go to www.pjgray.com.